The door behind her slowly opened, a chill breeze coming from inside the house. "What are you doing, Mommy?" asked the thing she now knew wasn't Charlie. It was the spirit of her dead son Michael, infused with evil. The killer of nearly her entire family.

She almost couldn't bear to look at this thing that had taken the image of her much-loved son. Now that she knew what it was, it looked less like Charlie.

As if hearing her thoughts, an unearthly wind suddenly ruffled the spirit's hair, and its mouth twitched, mocking her.

Instinctively she picked up Golda's knife and held it before her, long forgotten words rising to her mind, her voice weakly chanting. . .

Voyager

THE ⊗ FILES™

The Calusari

Novelization by Garth Nix

Based on the television series
The X-Files created by
Chris Carter

Based on the teleplay
written by Sara Charno

HarperCollins*Publishers*

Voyager
An Imprint of HarperCollins*Publishers*
77–85 Fulham Palace Road,
Hammersmith, London W6 8JB

This paperback edition 1997
1 2 3 4 5 6 7 8 9

First published in the USA by HarperTrophy
A division of HarperCollins*Publishers* 1997

ISBN 0 00 648324 0

Set in Goudy

Printed and bound in Australia by
Griffin Paperbacks, Netley, South Australia

Chapter One

The train whistled as it rounded the corner, the half-size red locomotive steaming powerfully, the brass fittings gleaming. All the children aboard were laughing and waving, happy to be at Lincoln Park.

A dark-haired boy stood by the fence that bordered the railroad track, watching the miniature train go past without any sign of enjoyment. A pink helium balloon bobbed above his head, held there by a silver string clutched in the boy's hand.

"Charlie!"

Someone called his name, and he turned to look. His mother, Maggie Holvey, beckoned him over. His younger brother, Teddy, was next to her, his bright blond hair shining. He was laughing, a happy child, so different from

Charlie with his sullen expression. Teddy held another balloon by a silver string, and his mother held him by a leash attached to the harness securely buckled around his little two-year-old body.

"Come on, Charlie," called Maggie, her voice colored with the Romanian accent that had not disappeared after nearly ten years in America. Until she spoke, she seemed like any other American mom.

Charlie, watching Teddy, didn't respond. Suddenly Teddy smiled and waddled away from Maggie, reaching out to someone approaching through the passing crowd of parents and children. Their father, Steve Holvey, was coming over, carefully balancing two ice-cream cones in each hand.

"Charlie . . . Hey! Ice cream!" Steve called out. But even ice cream didn't seem to interest Charlie. Face devoid of any emotion, the balloon bobbing along above his head, he walked over to join his father, mother, and brother.

Unlike Charlie, Teddy really did want the

ice cream, and reached for it too soon. Walking was still something fairly new for him, and the combination of balloon and ice cream too difficult. With a wail he fell forward, smearing ice cream over a face suddenly crumpled, smile gone in an instant. His balloon slipped through his fingers, streaking up into the sky, to be taken off northward by the wind.

"Shush, Teddy. Don't cry," soothed Maggie, picking up her younger son. "We'll get you another balloon, honey."

Promises don't mean much to a two-year-old. Teddy kept on bawling, tears mixing with the chocolate ice cream on his face. Without thinking, Steve grabbed Charlie's balloon and handed it to Teddy.

"Look. Here's your balloon."

Magically Teddy stopped in mid-bawl, once the string was safe in his pudgy hand and the pink balloon was floating above him. Charlie watched, a flicker of some emotion passing across his face for the first time.

"Such a mess!" exclaimed Maggie, looking

down at her small, chocolate-stained son. "We have to get you cleaned up. Steven . . ."

"Yeah, sure . . . go on. Charlie and I will wait for you," replied Steve, sighing with relief that catastrophe had been so easily averted. Realizing he was still holding three ice creams, he offered one to Charlie.

"Eat your ice cream before it melts."

Charlie didn't move, hands still at his sides, ignoring the cone held out to him.

"I want my balloon."

"Yeah. Okay. We'll get you another one . . ."

"No," said Charlie vehemently. "I want *my* balloon."

"Fine, we'll get you another balloon!" exclaimed Steve, but Charlie still wouldn't take the ice cream. Finally Steve shrugged and tossed all three cones into a nearby trash can, muttering about the waste of money. If it wasn't one kid spoiling their day out, it was the other . . .

The park bathrooms were very basic. All stainless steel and concrete, the sinks were bolted to the wall and held up by steel posts. Maggie finished wiping off Teddy's face, then tied his halter leash to the sink stand and checked the knot to make sure it couldn't come undone.

"Okay, Teddy. I'll be right out." She smiled down at him before entering a stall and closing the door.

As it clicked shut, Teddy let go of the balloon, happily watching it float to the ceiling and bounce there, unable to escape into the open air.

There was a gap under the stall door, and Maggie bent down to look through it as she sat, reassured by the sight of Teddy's little legs all wrapped up in bulky blue trousers. She started to sing, to reassure him that she was close by.

"There were six in the bed and the little one said, 'Roll over . . . roll over . . .' "

But Teddy wasn't listening to her singing. He was watching the balloon. It had suddenly begun to move, as if pulled down by an invisible force. Lower and lower it came; then it moved out—toward the outside door. As it reached the door frame, the toilet flushed.

Maggie kept singing as she tucked her shirt back into her jeans.

"There were five in the bed and the little one said, 'Roll over . . . roll over . . .' "

She ducked down again to see Teddy's legs for a second, and kept singing as she unlocked the door.

"They all rolled over and one fell . . ."

She opened the door and the singing stopped, her mouth open, no sound coming out. Teddy's halter was hanging from the sink. Empty. There was no sign of her precious child.

Or the balloon.

Panicked, Maggie dashed for the door, already shouting.

"Teddy! Teddy!"

Teddy wasn't far away, but he didn't hear her. All his concentration was on the balloon that floated just ahead of him, always out of reach. He was stumbling along as fast he could go, little arms reaching out. But always as his fingers closed, the silver string jumped away and the balloon led him farther on—down the lawn, and through the whitewashed gate that was open just enough for him to slide through. Finally the balloon stopped and Teddy smiled, reaching up for it . . .

Only Charlie saw the little boy cross the fence. His dark eyes were wide open, piercing the crowd, his father standing unaware beside him. But Charlie didn't say anything, didn't suddenly shout. He didn't do anything you'd expect from a boy seeing his little brother lost and wandering . . . wandering into danger.

Back on the lawn a man bent over his camera, looking through the viewfinder at his wife and children posing with one of the park's people-size animals. This one was a pink pig, even pinker than the cotton candy his children were smearing all over themselves. Satisfied with the shot, he clicked the shutter and looked up, his eye suddenly focusing on a very small child and a pink balloon in the background.

For a second he didn't think about where the child was; then the whistle of the miniature train—suddenly closer than it had been—made him realize.

"There's a kid on the tracks!" he shouted.

Steve was only a few yards away when he heard the shout, back at the balloon stand with Charlie. He wheeled around to look, a terrible stab of fear hitting him in the gut as he saw the blue suit and the pink balloon. It was Teddy, standing on the train tracks—and the train was already rounding the last corner, steaming at full speed toward his boy.

"Oh my God!" he groaned, already starting to run, a shout then exploding out of him: "Stop the train!"

Maggie, looking through the crowd at knee level, heard his shout and instinctively knew that Teddy was in danger. She started running toward her husband's voice.

Steve ran, his mind refusing to acknowledge the fact that he couldn't make it in time. The train was too close and Teddy just wasn't moving. Desperately he shouted again, willing his son to move, just a few feet, just a few inches, off the track . . .

"Teddy! Get off the tracks!"

Charlie followed him at a walk, still watching his brother. Charlie seemed in no hurry, as if he knew he would arrive at just the right time to see whatever would be seen.

Inside the locomotive the driver smiled back at his passengers. He'd been picked to drive the train because he looked like an old-time engineer in his Casey Jones hat and he could smile nicely. That smile vanished in a flash as he looked ahead and saw the child standing on the tracks, oblivious to the train's approach. Instantly his hand shot out to pull the emergency brake, but it had no effect on the train. He tried the brake again, but there was nothing, and the kid still hadn't even looked. Reaching up, he pulled the whistle cord again and again, the shrill noise blaring out, drowning the calls of the adults as they ran toward the tracks. Surely the kid would hear . . .

Teddy hummed the "Roll over" song and pulled at the balloon, happy that he had it back again. He didn't hear the whistle, or the shouts.

He never knew when the train hit him, whistle still blowing as it ended his short life.

"No!" screamed Steve as the red blur of the train passed just in front of him and Teddy went under, the pink balloon caught for an instant before the sharp wheels cut the silver string and it snapped away.

Then the train was gone and Maggie was there, hands held to her mouth to try to stifle the scream that waited to burst forth. Behind her, other parents used their hands, too, shielding their children's eyes, turning them away from the awful scene on the railway tracks.

Only Maggie went forward, kneeling down to pick up her dead child, cradling him as if she might somehow bring him back to life with her love. Steve, face blank with shock, looked on, unable to move or speak.

Back in the crowd, Charlie watched too, his face as expressionless as it had been all day. His father hadn't had time to buy him another balloon, but there was one floating behind him now, trailing a shredded piece of string. Untethered, it hung in midair. Almost as if it were held there, waiting. . .

Chapter Two

The photograph filled the entire projection screen, showing a woman and two kids with cotton-candy sticks half as big as they were, posing with a guy in a pink pig suit.

Special Agent Dana Scully looked at the projection, waiting for her partner to explain why he'd brought her down to this lab at Georgetown University to see a photograph. Whatever it was, she knew that Special Agent Fox Mulder would have a weird explanation for it. This might look like a normal family enjoying themselves at an amusement park, but there had to be more to it for Mulder to get interested.

And why did they have to come down to this guy's lab to look at the photo? He was another one of Mulder's friends who specialized in who-knew-what, though the tons of electronic equipment, video, and camera gear sure looked impressive.

As Scully expected, it wasn't the obvious part of the photo Mulder was interested in. Leaning forward, he pointed at a small figure, behind the family, on the other side of a white fence.

"This photo was taken in an amusement park three months ago," Mulder explained. "The young boy in the background is Teddy Holvey, two years old. He was killed just seconds after this was taken."

"How?" asked Scully.

"According to the police report, Teddy wandered onto the tracks of a miniature train. The conductor was unable to stop in time—there was a malfunction in the braking system."

"Teddy's father works for the State Department," Mulder continued, handing Scully a file. "A coroner's inquest was held due to the unusual circumstances surrounding the accident."

Scully quickly flipped through the coroner's report, still wondering exactly what Mulder was about to spring on her.

"And did the inquest turn up anything unusual?"

"No," replied Mulder. "But the county medical examiner called me afterward. He was troubled by the case. And by this photograph. With good reason, I think."

Scully looked at him curiously, and then back at the photograph. What had she missed?

"That's a helium balloon. One thing I learned in kindergarten is that if you let them go, they float up, up, and away. But this balloon is moving away from him . . . horizontally . . . like it's being pulled."

"Didn't you learn about wind in kindergarten?" asked Scully, in the tone of voice Mulder knew meant she wasn't buying this.

"I called the National Weather Service. And they said on the day that Teddy died the wind was blowing north. The balloon is moving south, as if it's being pulled against the wind."

"Pulled? By whom?"

"I don't know," said Mulder thoughtfully. "That's why I came to Chuck Burk. The king of digital imaging."

He looked over at the man sitting at the computer, who put down his coffee and rested his hands on the keyboard in front of him. Scully nodded. Now she knew what the guy was an expert in, and catalogued him among Mulder's sources.

"He can extract incredibly small details from a simple photographic print," continued Mulder, obviously impressed at his friend's expertise.

"Not details," said Chuck, with a scientist's pedantry. "Information. Check the monitor."

He typed in a few commands as Mulder and Scully moved closer together to get a good view of the monitor. It showed the same photograph, but centered on Teddy and his balloon. Chuck kept hitting keys and the image changed color as he enhanced it.

"We have limitations on how much information the eye can perceive unaided," he lectured as he tapped away. "Using special software I've designed, we can detect 'hidden' information, manipulate it—and we can enhance it."

Switching to the mouse, he moved it a few times and clicked.

"Watch right here. There it is."

The monitor changed for the last time, and Scully leaned forward to watch more closely. There now seemed to be a vaguely human shape—about twice as big as Teddy—actually holding the balloon, dragging it away from the boy.

"It's clearly a concentration of electromagnetic energy," said Mulder, pointing at the screen.

"You're saying a ghost killed Teddy Holvey?" asked Scully.

Mulder and Chuck looked at her, their faces acknowledging that this was exactly what they thought.

"Has anyone bothered to check the camera that took this photo? The lens, or the film?"

"It all checked out, Scully," affirmed Mulder,

passing her an evidence bag with the camera in question. "I think from the information here, this is clearly some kind of poltergeist activity."

Scully looked at him and back at the monitor, doubt in her voice. "Mulder, this 'information' is a result of the same phenomenon that produces newspaper photos with Jesus's face in the foliage of an elm tree. A chance occurrence of light and shadow."

Mulder looked at her and got another evidence bag off the shelf to build up his case. Scully never did take his leaps of intuition without heavy-duty supporting facts.

"To get onto those railroad tracks, Teddy Holvey had to escape this childproof halter his mother had tied to a bathroom sink."

"I've seen some pretty slippery two-year-olds," commented Scully, unconvinced.

"So the county medical examiner put it on his own two-year-old, and it was physically impossible for the kid to reach around and free himself. So unless Teddy Holvey was the reincarnation of Houdini . . ."

The Holveys lived in a large colonial-style house in Arlington, Virginia. A white house, set in the middle of a well-maintained garden with a front lawn, trees, and hedges.

An old woman was looking out one of the upstairs windows, her wrinkled face framed by a black woolen scarf almost like a hood. Half her view was obscured by a rectangular piece of glass art stuck to the window. Made up of red-and-gold stained glass, it was cleverly put together to show the design of a reverse swastika, with four dots inside each spoke.

She looked like a peasant woman from the Old World, from some remote village in Central Europe. Someone who had seen much harshness in her life, and perhaps considerable evil. A perfect extra for a horror film.

Now she was watching a car roll up and park outside the house. Two people got out. A man and a woman, both in suits and overcoats. They had that indefinable air about them that said "police," or "government."

The old woman knew they wouldn't understand. She stopped looking, and turned away into the darkness of her room.

Mulder and Scully continued walking up to the house, unaware that they had been watched, judged—and found wanting. They knocked on the front door.

Chapter Three

It was dark in the Holveys' living room, despite the warm red glow of the fire and the lamps on either side of the fireplace. Steve and Maggie Holvey sat uncomfortably on the sofa, with Mulder sitting opposite them. Scully stood near the door, her attention partly tuned to what might be going on in the rest of the house. Both FBI agents had kept their coats on, perhaps feeling an indefinable chill. The Holveys didn't seem to feel the cold.

Maggie Holvey was clearly uneasy, and uncertain as to why Mulder and Scully were there.

"I don't understand. There was already a formal inquest," she said.

"We're here apart from that investigation,"

Mulder explained, as watchful as ever, observing them as much as listening to their answers. "We have reason to believe there's something that may have been overlooked."

"Like what?" asked Maggie, puzzled and still defensive.

Mulder didn't try to make what he was going to say any easier.

"The possibility that Teddy may have been led onto the tracks."

"Oh my God," murmured Maggie, looking as if she might once again be seeing Teddy's body dead on the cold steel rails. Steve leaned toward her, reaching out with a comforting hand.

"There were over a hundred witnesses," Steve exclaimed. "We saw Teddy ourselves . . ."

As he spoke, the fire suddenly flared, the flames leaping up to twice their height—and Charlie appeared silently in the doorway. Mulder noted his presence, warning Scully with a slight nod of his head. She looked, too, but the boy ducked back into the hallway.

As he left, the fire died back down.

Steve hadn't noticed, and just kept on talking. "He was chasing a balloon. There was no one else around. It was an awful accident. But that's all it was."

"Do you have any reason to believe someone would want to hurt Teddy?" asked Mulder.

"He was just a little boy," said Maggie. "Why would anyone want to hurt him?"

Scully listened to her answer as she moved out of the room, following Charlie. She only had to look around the door to see him. He was halfway up the stairs, next to an old lady who was muttering something to him and drawing on the back of his hand with a red pen.

Scully took this in impassively, also noting the red string tied around the boy's wrist. Then she stepped back to hear what was going on inside, focusing her attention on the parents. Some questions were forming in her mind, and she didn't like the direction her thoughts were taking.

"Look, I don't know what you're getting

at," Steve was saying. "We loved Teddy. If you're suggesting that we had anything to do with this—you're way out of line."

"Mrs. Holvey, did you hear anything in the bathroom before Teddy disappeared?" asked Mulder.

"I already told them at the inquest. I heard nothing."

Scully reentered the room, firing off her first question. She didn't show her feelings to the Holveys, but Mulder's swift glance told him that she was getting a feel for the case.

"Mrs. Holvey, at the time of the accident did you have any hired help?" she asked.

"No. My mother came to live with us when Teddy was born."

Mulder was in next, following his own line of questioning.

"At the time of Teddy's death, had you witnessed anything odd at all in the house? Things moving? Strange objects appearing? Anything like—"

He was cut off as a shrill whistle suddenly sounded all through the house. Steve was up like a shot, hurrying from the room.

"It's that damned smoke detector. I'll be right back."

A few seconds later the scream of the smoke detector stopped—and all the lights suddenly winked out, leaving darkness and the red glow of the fire.

"Does this happen often?" Mulder queried, leaning forward to look at Maggie, her face half lit by the leaping flames, half in shadow.

"It's an old house." She shrugged. "We sometimes have problems with the wiring."

Then the lights came back on—revealing the old woman standing in the room, holding Charlie's hand.

"It's the devil! The devil!" the woman cried in Romanian.

"Mother, it's a false alarm," replied Maggie in English, trying to calm her. She hoped the FBI agents didn't speak any Romanian, and would not understand her mother's wild accusations.

"The boy is evil! Evil!" the old woman continued, still in Romanian. A harsh tongue, totally unfamiliar to Mulder and Scully, who stared at her. Mulder, as always, was taking in everything about her and the boy. Including the reverse swastika with four dots drawn in red on the back of the boy's hand.

"Mother!" exclaimed Maggie.

"What is she saying?" asked Scully as Steve came into the room, looking as if his mother-in-law's outburst was the last thing he needed on top of everything else.

"Maggie!" Steve's voice was troubled as he entreated her to control her mother. But the old woman was not to be stopped. Switching to broken English, she made a proclamation.

"You marry devil, you have devil child!"

That said, she turned away, leading Charlie out. The two FBI agents and the weary couple watched her for a few seconds, awkwardness hanging over them all.

"I'm sorry," said Steve finally. "This is a bad time."

Chapter Four

The events of the evening before had fired both FBI agents' particular thought processes and led them along their own lines of inquiry, each following up different clues from the visit to the Holvey house.

Mulder was in the middle of his research when Scully dropped in to his office. Leaning back in his chair, unconscious of the fact that he was framed by the "I Want to Believe" poster behind him on the wall, he held open the book he was reading to show Scully a familiar symbol.

"Recognize this?" he asked.

"Sure. It's a swastika."

"Also known as a gammadion or a fylfot. It's an ancient sign of good luck or protection used by various cultures since the Middle Ages."

"And?" prompted Scully.

"And the Holveys' son had one on the back of his hand last night. My guess is it was drawn there by the old lady. To protect him."

"You're right. I saw her drawing it."

"And you didn't think that was strange?" asked Mulder, surprised that Scully hadn't reacted more to this development. Or told him.

"No. I think that child needs all the protection he can get. Just not from ghosties or beasties. Take a look at this."

Scully countered Mulder's book of superstitions by handing him the first of her two files. Teddy Holvey's medical record. Hard, scientific data. Mulder took it and looked up at her inquiringly.

"Have you ever heard of Munchausen by proxy?" she asked.

"Yeah." Mulder smiled. "My grandfather used to take that for his stomach."

Scully ignored his attempt at humor. They rarely laughed together, and Mulder didn't often try even the beginning of a joke. Perhaps he was unconsciously relieved that this wasn't going to be an X-file, Scully thought. She was convinced there was a far more mundane, if still unpleasant, explanation.

"It's when a parent or caretaker brings harm to a child by inducing medical symptoms," she continued. "Usually as a way of gaining attention or status. If you take a look at Teddy Holvey's medical history, you'll see he was admitted to various hospitals ten times during the two years he was alive. That's once every three months."

Mulder opened the file and flipped through it, reading aloud as he went.

"Projectile vomiting at three months, diarrhea at four months, vomiting, diarrhea, diarrhea . . ."

"Each time, the doctors were unable to determine the cause of the illness," Scully pointed out, confident she was on the right track.

"And no one questioned this?" asked Mulder, impressed even if it wasn't the explanation he was looking for.

"Well, the family moved around a lot because of Steve's job. Records take time to transfer from one hospital to another—but this kind of abuse isn't usually limited to just one child, so I checked out Charlie's records too."

Scully handed Mulder the second file as she continued talking. He opened it, starting to think that maybe Scully really did have a rational, scientific explanation this time.

"Charlie had health problems too?" he asked.

"Ever since his brother was born," confirmed Scully. "Right after Maggie Holvey's mother came to live with them."

Mulder looked down at the file again, noting the dates, concern showing on his normally impassive face.

"Often the perpetrator of Munchausen by proxy views the child as evil. The old woman would be a likely candidate. But it could be any family member."

Mulder nodded. This definitely needed to be checked out.

"Do you feel like a walk over to the State Department, Scully?"

Steve Holvey's office had State Department written all over it. The wood-paneled walls, the plaques commemorating service in foreign countries, the plush red armchairs and ordered filing cabinets were a far cry from Mulder's cluttered FBI office. Steve Holvey sat behind his desk, struggling to find the answers Mulder and Scully were looking for. Sun leaked through the closed blinds behind him, glinting off the visitor badges worn by the two FBI agents.

"Things have been strained since Golda— my mother-in-law—moved in with us," Steve began hesitantly. "I met Maggie in Romania in 1984. Golda forbade our marriage. Said I was the devil . . . after I was transferred back to the U.S., things got somewhat better. Until Teddy was born and she came to live with us. That's when the strangeness really started."

"What kind of strangeness?" asked Mulder.

He still had the feeling that there was more to the picture, that some facts were escaping him. It just didn't add up, no matter how Scully saw it.

Steve hesitated, unsure of how to go on. But it was all going to come out now anyway . . .

"Superstitions rule Golda's life. She'll spit when anyone compliments the kids. Once she moved in with us, she started pouring hot water over the threshold to ward off demons, tying red strings around the kids' wrists. One day I caught her throwing chicken guts on the roof. Then Teddy and Charlie started getting sick . . . a lot."

"And you suspect Golda?" questioned Scully, trying to get him to say what he was clearly thinking.

"She calls Charlie evil, right to his face. But at the same time she dotes on him. Like she's afraid of him."

"Afraid *of* him, or *for* him?" interjected Mulder.

"I just don't know . . ."

Scully chose that moment to ask a question she'd been waiting to ask.

"Are you familiar with Munchausen by proxy, Mr. Holvey?"

From the look of shock on Steve's face, he clearly did know what Munchausen by proxy was—and his next words confirmed it.

"Are you accusing us of child abuse?"

"Teddy's medical records have raised some questions," Scully explained. It was pretty clear she suspected somebody of child abuse.

Steve looked down at his desk, struggling with something he didn't want to even acknowledge, let alone bring out into the open.

"I could never say this to Maggie," he said hesitantly. "But I've wondered if it wasn't Golda who snuck in and let Teddy out of the bathroom that day."

"I'd like to interview your son," said Scully, leaning forward and handing Steve a business card. "With a professional counselor present."

Steve took the card, eyes quickly scanning the type: KAREN KOSSEFF, L.C.S.W, PSYCHIATRIC

SOCIAL WORKER, FEDERAL BUREAU OF INVESTI-
GATION.

"Oh boy," he said, dread in his voice. "This
is going to be hard."

Chapter Five

Charlie sat at the blue-tiled table in the kitchen, watching his grandmother stir a pot of canned spaghetti on the stove. His parents were arguing in the living room, but he gave no sign that he could hear them. It was impossible to guess what was going on inside his head.

Mulder was listening to them, though, as he stood in the doorway keeping an eye on the boy. Scully was listening too, and watching the old woman carefully. The grandmother was still the number-one suspect in Scully's opinion. Steve's remarks back at the State Department had only strengthened her suspicions.

Steve had started by pleading with Maggie, but it wasn't any use, and their disagreement began building to a full-scale argument.

"What do they want?" she asked, tension adding volume to her voice. "To take Charlie away from us?"

"They just want him to talk to the social worker," Steve explained patiently. "She's expecting us."

"Social worker? No! She'll put ideas in Charlie's head!"

"You're being unreasonable —" Steve started to say, but Maggie wasn't listening.

"You want to take him away from me. You blame me for Teddy, and now you want to take Charlie away from me!"

"I'm not going to listen to this!" exclaimed Steve, finally exasperated beyond endurance. "This is ridiculous! If you want to come, you can, but I'm taking Charlie now."

Suddenly Maggie's anger changed to fear, and it was her turn to plead.

"No, Steven. He is my son . . ."

Listening to them argue had almost distracted Scully, but she still saw Golda pull a small paper packet from a pocket in her skirt and sprinkle some sort of powder in the food she was preparing for Charlie. As Steve and Maggie came back into the kitchen, the old woman quickly moved across with the plate, as if she needed to get Charlie to eat it before he went away. Scully intercepted her, asking, "What is that?"

Golda stopped and looked up at her angrily.

"You excite the devil here!" she hissed. The Romanian words were meaningless to Scully, but the old woman's intentions were clear. It was obvious that she thought Scully was stepping into something she didn't understand.

Scully started to ask her another question, but Steve interrupted.

"Come on, Charlie. Let's get your coat," he instructed his son, dropping his hands onto Charlie's shoulders as if to make it clear that he was in charge of the boy.

Maggie was close on his heels, arms folded across her chest, holding her anger in check. She glared at Steve and the two FBI agents.

"You have no right to do this!" she declared.

"Maggie!" Steve warned, that single word making it clear he wasn't going to back down. Still with one hand on Charlie's shoulder, he gave the boy a nudge toward the door to the garage, and Maggie knew that there was nothing more she could do. Charlie was going to see the social worker.

"Come on," Steve said to Mulder and Scully. "We'll meet you out front."

Maggie watched them go, then stormed up the stairs. Scully paused to look back at the old woman in the kitchen. For some reason Golda had lost her haughty look and wouldn't meet Scully's eyes, turning to face the cupboards. In fact, she seemed almost . . . afraid.

Outside the house, Mulder and Scully watched the Holveys' garage, ready to follow Steve to Karen Kosseff's office. The garage door wasn't open yet; Scully half expected to see Golda or Maggie come through the front door in some last-minute effort to prevent Charlie from meeting the social worker.

x   x   x

Inside the garage, Steve and Charlie got in the car and buckled their seat belts, Steve checking to make sure Charlie had done it right. It was a routine they'd both followed many times before.

"Okay. You buckled in there?"

"Yeah," said Charlie perfunctorily. He didn't seem to care where they were going; he just stared out the windshield. Hardly blinking, as if his eyes saw something distant and far off, way beyond the wall of the garage.

Steve nodded and reached up to press the button on the automatic garage-door opener stuck to the sun visor. Nothing happened, so Steve pressed it again, and then for a third time—but the door still didn't move.

"Dammit!" he exclaimed, unbuckling and getting out of the car. Smoke detectors, bad wiring, and now the damn garage-door opener! Shaking his head, he dragged the stepladder over and climbed up to the ceiling to take a look at the motor that drove the automatic door. There was a reset switch up there somewhere, but where was it? Craning his neck to get a good look at the side of the motor, he didn't notice his tie hanging back over his shoulder . . . draped over the drive chain . . .

Suddenly there was a *thwick* below him as the automatic lock mechanism activated in the car . . . and Charlie was jolted out of his private world, coming suddenly alert, throwing himself across the seat to look out the driver's side at his father.

Then the garage-door motor started up.

Instantly the chain began to move, catching Steve's tie in the cog. At the tug on his neck he looked surprised, then suddenly afraid, as the motor kept on dragging his tie. Tightening it, strangling him. Desperate, he reached up to try and pull it free, his feet kicking and flailing . . .

"No! Stop! Daddy! Daddy!" screamed Charlie as his father's feet beat against the rear passenger window, safety glass crumbling in beneath the kicks of the choking man. Tears were running down Charlie's face as he beat against his own window uselessly, screaming, "Stop! Daddy! Daddy!"

But still the motor wound on, till the garage door was almost fully open and Steve Holvey's kicks were getting weaker and weaker, his life slowly strangled from him.

Scully saw him first as the garage door flipped up, shouting "Mulder" as she flung the car door open. A few seconds later both agents were sprinting up to the garage, Mulder grabbing Steve's legs to try and prop him up. But it was too late. One look at his blood-flushed face and popping eyes told Mulder the man was dead.

Scully looked too, then swiftly back at the boy in the locked car. Tears were streaming down his cheeks, the terror of his father's death showing clearly in his frightened eyes. The impassive mask Charlie had always worn before was completely gone. He almost looked like a different boy . . .

Chapter Six

It was night again at the Holvey house. A cold, dark night, a fitting end to the day that had seen the strange death of Steve Holvey. The second death in the family within three months. To lose a baby son and a husband so close together would be a cruel blow to anyone, thought Scully, looking in on Maggie Holvey. There was a doctor with her in her bedroom now, treating her for shock.

Two uniformed officers were in the hall, writing up a report. One of them peered through a darkened door. As Scully walked toward them, he met her eyes. Obviously he didn't like whatever he'd just spotted.

"You see this?" asked the officer, pointing inside the room. *The old woman's bedroom,* Scully remembered. Golda. Probably the closest thing to a witch she'd met since the fairy tales of her childhood.

She went in.

Many candles lit the room, yellow tongues of light flickering, tasting the darkness. Heavy curtains were bunched on either side of the windows, hinting that they were opened only at night, as if daylight could never be allowed to enter. A central table held a brass bowl surrounded by antique bottles full of strange herbs and stranger liquids.

Scully went closer, a white shape dimly seen in the candlelight grabbing her attention, a darker shadow next to it. They couldn't be dead chickens, surely? But they were. One black, one white. Dead roosters, their throats cut, limp bodies drained of blood. Some of the blood was in the bowl.

A noise outside distracted Scully, and she carefully skirted the table to look out the window. There was the reverse swastika again, red-stained glass on gold, in a wooden frame. Hanging in the window, as if the old woman believed it would keep some evil out. Or keep it in. Obviously superstition had a strong hold on Golda's mind.

Not on Scully's, though. Something fiercely scientific and rational anchored her mind against the stuff Mulder had no difficulty in believing. Even when weird things happened, Scully could somehow deal with it and keep herself mentally insulated.

Not that the noise outside was anything weird. Just car doors opening, Scully saw. A station wagon had pulled up and Golda was greeting the people getting out. Three men, all dressed in black, with white-collared shirts buttoned to the neck without ties. And they were wearing odd broad-brimmed black hats. Like priests, or perhaps some strange variety of undertaker.

Presumably Romanians, Scully thought, brought in by the old woman. Serious-looking people, particularly the man who was obviously their leader. Old and white-haired, he had an equally white beard, like a prophet out of the Bible. He was listening to Golda and she was pointing back to the house.

The more she saw, the more Scully knew that Charlie didn't belong in this home. Turning on her heel, she went to make a call, suppressing the smallest of shudders as she left the room that reeked of superstition.

Down in the garage, Mulder finished wiping some strange ash off the motor with his latex-gloved hands, collecting it in an evidence bag. Unlike Steve Holvey's, his tie was safely tucked into his shirt. The garage door was closed again, and Mulder wasn't taking any chances with whatever had started the motor up last time.

Scully came in as he climbed down the ladder.

"Find anything?" she asked him.

"Yeah," replied Mulder, offering her the bag. "Maybe."

"It looks like ash."

"Yeah," confirmed Mulder, running his gloved hand over the roof of the late Steve Holvey's car, dislodging more ash. "Look at this—it's everywhere."

"The Holveys said earlier that they had some problems with the wiring of this house," Scully offered in explanation. "It could be from the motor shorting out."

"I checked the motor. It's in perfect working order."

"So what do you think it is?"

"I don't know," Mulder replied thoughtfully. "I'm going to have it analyzed."

Whatever the ash was, it seemed irrelevant to Scully. There were more important things to take care of.

"Well, I think before we do anything we have to get Charlie Holvey out of the house. I just put a call in to a social worker to come out and make a report."

"The courts are reluctant to intervene in these matters," Mulder pointed out. His fascination with the unexplained hadn't dulled his attention to the more worldly details of his job as an FBI agent.

"Not if the child is in danger," argued Scully. "And not after they see the two dead roosters in the old woman's bedroom."

"Really?" asked Mulder. Somehow this case didn't add up yet. This strange ash, the old woman's fixation with evil . . .

"Do you still think this is Munchausen by proxy, Scully?"

Scully was quick to confirm her belief. "Without a doubt."

Almost before the last word was out of her mouth, the motor above their heads sprang to life and the garage door began to rise, startling them both.

"What did you do?" asked Scully.

"I didn't do anything," Mulder said slowly, looking out at the driveway. There were people standing there, revealed as the door rose higher. Golda, with Charlie in front of her, flanked by the three men Scully had seen from the window.

"Stay . . . away . . . from . . . our . . . home," Golda declared in halting English. She backed up this warning with a stony glare and turned away, pushing Charlie in front of her. The black-clad men followed after her silently.

Chapter 7

Scully was at Mulder's desk, reading over the file on the Holveys, waiting for him to get back with the X-ray photoelectron spectrograph of the ash. It was probably some natural phenomenon, of course, but Mulder seemed to expect it to be something peculiar.

She looked up as he came back in, brandishing a piece of graph paper.

"Want to see something weird?" he asked, handing over the graph. To someone who knew him as well as Scully did, it was clear he was excited, though you wouldn't be able to tell by his expression. Just the way he moved, the sudden quickening in his actions.

"What?" asked Scully. It was simply a straight line plotted on a piece of graph paper.

"It's the chem-lab analysis of the ash from the Holvey house," Mulder explained hurriedly, grabbing his coat from the back of the chair. Flicking it over his shoulder, he pointed back at the graph, at the straight line.

"No trace of any metal. No trace of carbon, or oxygen. No nothing."

"What do you mean?" asked Scully, puzzled.

"It doesn't contain anything organic or inorganic. In fact, according to the technicians, this ash doesn't exist. Come on!"

"Where are we going?" asked Scully, jumping up from the desk. Whatever this ash was . . . or wasn't, it had certainly stirred up Mulder.

"To get a second opinion," replied Mulder, already halfway out the door.

The second opinion Mulder wanted turned out to be Chuck Burk's, which meant another visit to Georgetown University and the lab full of video and other more esoteric electronic equipment.

Chuck took the small bag of ash almost reverently, fingering it with care, looking down through his horn-rimmed glasses as if he didn't really believe what he was seeing.

"Oh, wow! I haven't seen this for a while . . . not since India, 1979."

"India?" asked Scully, her earlier doubts about this guy resurfacing. Mulder sure could pick his "technical" experts.

"Before he succumbed to academia, Chuck did a tour of duty on the old hippie trail," Mulder replied.

"It's called *Vibuti*," explained Chuck. "Holy Ash. Technically it's known as an apport."

He made a sweeping gesture, fingers splayed out. "Something that materializes out of thin air."

"Wait a second," Scully intervened. "Nothing just materializes out of thin air."

"You've read the Bible," said Chuck, opening the bag to rub his thumb and forefinger through the ash. "You remember the story about Jesus creating the loaves and fishes . . ."

"But that's a parable."

"In 1979 I witnessed a guru named Sai Baba create an entire feast out of thin air."

"Too bad you didn't take a picture," Scully said, voice full of sarcasm. "You could have run it through your computer and seen the entire Last Supper."

Mulder laughed, amused at Scully's rejoinder. Chuck ignored Scully, continuing his explanation. She had the feeling that Chuck put up with her only for Mulder's sake.

"Vibuti is produced by the presence of spirit beings. Or during bilocation, which is a phenomenon in which a person's energy is transported to a different location."

"That energy could be what set off the garage-door opener," said Mulder.

Scully shook her head. "Yeah, that or somebody simply activated a remote control."

"Who are you suggesting did that?" asked Mulder.

"Who was standing there when the garage-door opener started unexpectedly on us yesterday?"

"The old lady," Mulder said. He paused, then added, "And Charlie."

He and Scully exchanged looks. Neither had seriously considered this possibility before— that Charlie might not be a victim . . . but a perpetrator.

Particularly since his father's death had so conveniently delayed his questioning . . . questioning that should be resumed as quickly as possible.

It was clearly time for Mulder and Scully to go back to the ill-starred Holvey house . . .

At that moment the boy they wanted to talk to had his ear pressed up against the keyhole of his grandmother's bedroom, listening. She was in there, along with the three men in black, the ones who had come before. Somehow it concerned him, and he wanted to know what was happening. He needed to know. He must know . . .

Inside, the heavy curtains had been drawn against the sun. Once again there was only the light of many candles. Golda and the three black-clad men—hatless now, red-and-black stoles draped over their shoulders—were gathered around the table in the center of the room, hands reaching out to the brass bowl. They were chanting, voices low and ominous, power gathering in their words.

"*Voi ilelor . . . maistrelor . . . dusmanele omenilor . . . stapinele vintulu . . . doamnele pamintulu . . . de prin vazduh sburati . . .*"

The chant continued as one of the men held up two dead roosters, blood from their slit necks dripping into the bowl. The old woman added herbs and dark liquids from the bottles and jars, the words of the chant building, focusing on the bowl.

"*Pe erbe lunecati . . . si pe valuri calcati . . . ve duceti in locuri . . . in balta tresti . . .*"

Now Golda lit a match, dropping the pale stick of wood and flame into the thick blood-rich mixture in the bowl. The match sank instantly, wood failing to float. She lit another and it sank too. Finally a third match fell flaming and was swallowed up.

Outside the door, Charlie began to sweat, his breathing becoming labored. Whatever was going on inside was tied to him, was affecting him. Blurring his vision, taking him out of himself . . .

The chant went on, and Golda raised a vial to add just a few drops of something rare and strange. As it fell into the bowl, the liquid suddenly boiled, a great column of steam billowing up—and in the steam, the head and naked torso of a boy appeared, body writhing, lips pulled back, eyes full of hate. It looked exactly like Charlie—but a Charlie warped and twisted by unspeakable evil.

The chanting grew louder, stronger, as if it had to grow more powerful in order to contain whatever was in the steam. And the image spoke too, in a voice deeper than Charlie's, speaking in Romanian, of which the boy knew only a few words.

"You have no power over us. You cannot

harm us!" the image snarled, anger almost physically striking at the four who sought to control it, as if by words alone it could command their destruction.

Downstairs, far away from the struggle in Golda's bedroom, someone knocked on the front door.

Chapter Eight

A middle-aged, professional-looking woman had knocked on the door several times. Finally it opened a little, to show the tired face of Maggie Holvey. She was wearing a gray bathrobe and looked like she had been dragged out of a much-needed afternoon nap.

"Mrs. Holvey?" said the visitor. "My name is Karen Kosseff. I'm a social worker from the FBI. I've been instructed to file a report for the court. Please, may I come in?"

Maggie shook her head wearily. "No. Please. I've had enough trouble."

"I understand, Mrs. Holvey," Kosseff said calmly, with the soothing voice of a professional helper. "But if you won't talk to me, I'm going to have to put that in my report, and it could very well complicate your situation."

Maggie hesitated, then gave way, opening the door to let the woman past.

Kosseff followed her in, glancing around at the hallway and up the wide staircase. It looked like a typical home for a mid-ranking government official's family.

Then she heard the plaintive cry of a small boy from somewhere above.

"Mommy!"

"Charlie . . . ?" cried Maggie in return, concern flashing into her face. Then she was off up the stairs, Kosseff following behind.

Charlie was lying in the hall, outside Golda's bedroom door. He looked feverish, disoriented, sweat soaking his shirt. Maggie rushed to him and cradled him in her arms.

"It's okay, Charlie. It's okay," she murmured, stroking his head. Realizing that the social worker was behind her, she quickly turned and said, "He's been sick. My mother was supposed to be looking after . . ."

She paused in mid-sentence, noticing a wisp of steam or smoke curling out from under her mother's door. Standing Charlie up as if they might both need to run away, she called out, "Mother. Mother!"

Without waiting for an answer, she opened the door—and saw the three men in their black suits, the ceremonial red-and-black stoles on their shoulders. Golda next to the brass bowl. The candles. The dead roosters. All the hallmarks of a ceremony she had heard about in her Romanian childhood. But had never seen . . . had never wanted to see . . .

The men looked at her, their eyes warning her to stay away. Golda was more forthright.

"Leave here at once!" she ordered in Romanian.

Maggie answered her in the same language, but directed her words at the men.

"Get out of my house."

They didn't move. The eldest, the man with the snowy beard, spoke with finality: "The boy is evil."

"Get out!" screamed Maggie, switching back to English, making herself unmistakably clear to Karen Kosseff as well as to the men.

The elder looked to Golda, who nodded.

Without further words, the men trailed out, removing their red-and-black stoles as they did so. Whatever ceremony they had begun was incomplete, but they left with the air of men who know there will be work to do later. It would not be finished here. The evil had not been defeated.

Maggie watched them go, then turned to her mother. Golda was moving toward her and the boy like an old crow advancing on a lamb.

"I have had enough, Mother," pronounced Maggie with desperate finality. "I want you out of my house."

Golda's answer came very fast.

"The boy's blood must be cleansed!" she spat, her bony hands reaching out to grab Charlie and drag him inside, the door slamming shut behind them. Shocked by the suddenness of the grab, Maggie could only beat against the door, screaming, "No, Mother! Mother!"

Kosseff saw it all, and she also saw the

wickedly curved knife in the middle of the table, steel shining in the candlelight. Training took over, and she ran downstairs for the phone.

Mulder and Scully were already parking out front, coming back to see if they could talk to Maggie about interviewing the boy. They didn't expect to see Karen Kosseff running out to meet them at the curb.

"Agent Scully!" she panted.

"What is it?" snapped Scully.

"Charlie Holvey. The grandmother's taken the child and locked him in the room with her. She has a knife. I've called 911."

"What happened?" asked Mulder as they jogged up between the neatly trimmed hedges toward the Holveys' front door.

"There were three strange men," Kosseff said hurriedly, obviously quite upset. "They were performing some kind of ritual . . ."

"Is the boy all right?" asked Scully.

Her answer came from upstairs. Charlie

was shouting something full of fear. It sounded like, "No! Don't!"

Instantly Mulder and Scully's jog turned into an all-out run, leaving Kosseff behind.

Inside the bedroom, all the candles went out, as if snuffed by the breath of some unseen spirit. Golda gasped, and held the boy to her with one hand, wielding the ceremonial knife in the other. Circling, she sliced at the air as if she could harm whatever malevolent force was beginning to manifest itself.

She knew she had only a few seconds to do what must be done. Grabbing Charlie's hand, she held his palm out and raised the knife, the sharp point descending to his bare skin. Flinching, he tried to pull away, scared by the sudden darkness, the knife . . .

"It is the only way, Mihai," she pleaded in her halting English . . . but Charlie slipped out of her grasp, retreating into the corner of the room. She grabbed at him . . . and missed. Before she could try again, something moved behind her. She whirled, raising the knife . . .

Too late, as a table suddenly hurtled through the air, smashing her to the floor.

Dazed by the blow, she felt for the knife, but it was lost. Looking up, fear filling her, fighting with the pain, she saw Charlie. Standing next to her, no longer afraid. His face was strange and sullen, and he held a dead rooster in each hand. One black. One white.

"You are too late to stop us," he said, in a voice that was not his own, speaking the Romanian he had never learned.

Golda screamed as he dropped the roosters and they came alive, pecking wildly at her face and neck, sharp beaks striking at her eyes . . .

Her scream didn't stop till Mulder smashed the door down. Guns drawn and ready, he and Scully found themselves facing only a small boy, his eyes blank and disoriented. Golda's body lay to one side, dead roosters next to it. Her face and neck bled from hundreds of tiny wounds.

Maggie saw her. She screamed, "Oh, no!"

and rushed to her side, Scully following more cautiously.

Mulder watched the boy. For just a second Mulder could have sworn that his face had changed, shifting under the skin, swimming into focus. But he couldn't be sure. Perhaps it was only a trick of the shadows in this strange, dark room . . .

Chapter Nine

Golda's bedroom seemed less odd when filled
with the people and procedures that followed
a modern-day death. Two paramedics were
zipping the old woman into a body bag on a
gurney, two uniformed police officers were
dusting for fingerprints, and a photographer
was taking pictures. It seemed a world apart
from the medieval implements of magic
strewn across the table, the dead roosters, the
heavy air of strangeness that had filled the
room . . .

Mulder was examining an old, crusted
bottle full of some herb that had fallen on the
carpet. He uncapped it and sniffed at the
herb, rising as Scully approached.

"Did you talk to Charlie?" he asked.

"He says he doesn't remember anything,"

replied Scully. "The coroner's preliminary report says the old woman died of a heart attack. But those wounds, Mulder . . . I would swear it looked like her eyes were pecked out."

"Well, there was more ash on the floor beneath her body, Scully. And look at this."

He showed her the herb bottle.

"What is it?"

"Mugwort. A ceremonial herb."

"Do you think this was a ritual killing?" Scully asked. Certain elements of this case were no longer fitting in with her theory of Munchausen by proxy.

"No." Mulder was definite. "The reverse swastika on the window, the red string on Charlie's wrist . . . they're all protective devices."

"Protection against what?"

"I don't know. But I think the old woman knew her family was in trouble and those men were performing a ritual to help her."

He paused as Maggie's voice rose up from downstairs. Angry and loud. Something in Romanian, then, more forcefully, in English.

"I want you out of my house!"

Scully looked at Mulder, and both moved to the door, the police officers following. It sounded like trouble brewing downstairs.

From the landing they could see Maggie facing the elder, his white beard bristling, voice strong and penetrating. Two other black-suited men stood behind him, looking equally intense. The old man was speaking in Romanian, one gnarled hand clutching at Maggie's arm, obviously trying to convince her of something.

"There is more to do," he told her. "You must let us finish! There is danger . . ."

Maggie replied in English, as if using this language would reduce the old man's power.

"I'm not interested in your superstition! Now get out! Now!"

The elder stared at her, then, catching sight of the FBI agents and the police, stared up at them for a moment, meeting Mulder's eyes. Their gaze locked briefly; then the elder turned away to leave, the other two preceding him out the door.

"Mrs. Holvey?" asked Scully, descending toward her.

"It's all right," Maggie reassured her.

"Who were they, Mrs. Holvey?" asked Mulder, still looking through the open door at the men walking to their car.

"They are the Calusari," said Maggie. She pronounced the word *Calu-SHAree*. "In Romania they are responsible for the correct observance of sacred rites."

"What was he saying?"

"He said it's not over," Maggie replied. She paused, and took a long, slow breath. "The evil is still here."

Mulder exchanged glances with Scully and moved quickly after the three men—after the Calusari.

The one who had been speaking—the one he thought of as the elder—was closest.

"Excuse me! Sir!" he called after them. "Can I have a word with you?"

The Calusari didn't turn around, but kept walking to their car. A brown station wagon, strangely incongruous for these priests—or sorcerers—or whatever they were.

"Sir, I'm with the FBI," Mulder continued as the other two men got in the car and the elder reached for his door handle. "I'd like to ask you some questions. You were trying to protect the family, weren't you? You said there was still evil here . . ."

The elder ignored him, opening the door.

"Sir, I can arrest you if I have to," Mulder warned. This made the elder stop, his door half open. Turning to face Mulder, fierce eyes hooded under the rim of his black hat, he spoke.

"The evil that is here has always been. It has gone by different names through history. Satan. Beelzebub. Lucifer. It doesn't care if it kills one boy or a million men."

The old man paused, then said with great force, "If you try to stop us . . . the blood will be on your hands."

With that, the elder stepped into the car and closed the door. The car pulled away from the curb, gently accelerating up the street. Mulder watched it go. Mentally he noted the license plate. He might need to talk further with the Calusari, to find out more about this "evil" that preyed upon the Holveys.

But first he needed to get more information from Maggie.

The Holveys' living room was a shrine to better days. The mantelpiece still boasted family photos. Steve and a pregnant Maggie, both smiling for the camera. All gone now. Maggie, face shut down with shock, stood in front of her happy past. Husband, son, and mother. All dead.

"Mrs. Holvey," Mulder began cautiously. "We know this is a difficult time, but there are questions that need to be answered."

"My mother used to say that evil follows evil," said Maggie, not really replying. Just talking to the space in front of her. "Once someone suffers a misfortune, they'll always have bad luck. I used to think it was just superstition. Now I don't know what to believe."

She focused on Mulder and Scully then, as if seeing them for the first time.

"I blamed her, you know. For all that's happened. I thought maybe she was putting a curse on us to punish me."

"Punish you for what?" asked Scully.

"For abandoning the old ways. I was raised to believe as she did—in spirits, the unseen world. When I married Steve and came to this country, I left all that behind."

"Do you know what ceremony your mother was trying to perform upstairs?" Mulder questioned.

"She was trying to cleanse the house of evil," Maggie said, in a distant and matter-of-fact tone. "She thought Charlie was responsible somehow . . ."

Her voice suddenly broke, her face falling. "How could he be responsible for all this horror? He's just a little boy."

Scully looked at Mulder, both clearly thinking the same thing. Somehow Charlie *was* the center of all this . . .

"Do you mind if we talk to Charlie about what happened in your mother's bedroom?" Scully asked.

It wasn't really a question. Things had gone too far for that. Still, Maggie tried to gather the strength to say no, to protect her son from this prying, this questioning. But it was too much. She was too tired, too broken by the events of recent days.

She nodded her assent.

Chapter Ten

Charlie had been taken to St. Matthew's Medical Center in Arlington. Ostensibly for observation following the fit or whatever it was he had had earlier that day, but also to allow him to be questioned by Karen Kosseff, the social worker.

She was with him now, in the hospital's playroom, which was full of toys and fun stuff for kids. Charlie sat on a cushion near a rocker in the shape of a fish. He was playing with an Etch-a-Sketch. Not really drawing anything. Just twiddling the knobs.

Mulder, Scully, and Maggie watched him from an adjoining room through a one-way mirror. Scully stood close to Maggie, worried that she might try to interrupt before they found out what they needed to know. The voices of Charlie and Kosseff came through an intercom, crackling slightly.

"Can you tell me about it?" asked Kosseff.

Charlie shook his head, not taking his eyes off the Etch-a-Sketch.

"Do you remember how you got there?" Kosseff pressed.

"No," said Charlie, after a long pause. He still wouldn't look at her.

"Your mother said you were there. Don't you remember?"

Charlie put down the Etch-a-Sketch and wandered over to a pile of toys. Kosseff followed him.

"I wasn't there!" Charlie protested.

"Many people saw you in the room," Kosseff continued patiently.

"I told you, it wasn't me!" Charlie suddenly screamed, kicking at the toys.

"Who was it then, Charlie?" asked Kosseff gently. "Who was in the room?"

Charlie began to breathe rapidly, chest heaving.

"No!"

"Was there someone else in the room?"

"No! I didn't hurt her!" screamed Charlie, breath coming in racking gasps, a tantrum building inside him.

"Charlie, who hurt your grandmother?"

"It was him," sobbed Charlie, backing away from the social worker as if he could see something she could not.

"Who, Charlie? Who?" Kosseff demanded urgently.

"It was Michael! Michael!" the boy screamed, falling down in a heap.

Maggie gasped, turning away from the agents, her hands going to her face as if she could somehow hide from whatever Charlie had just said.

"Mrs. Holvey?" Scully queried.

"We never told him," whispered Maggie. "It was agreed upon. It was our secret."

"What secret, Mrs. Holvey? What are you talking about?"

"Michael. He was Charlie's twin. He was . . . stillborn. Steven and I agreed never to tell Charlie about him."

This surprised even Mulder. He exchanged a quick look with Scully as Maggie came to an awful realization.

"My mother. She wanted to perform the ritual of separation when she heard of Michael's death . . . to divide their souls. She said if we didn't, the world of the dead would follow Charlie . . ."

She looked at Scully and Mulder, as if hoping they would affirm her next words.

"But it was just a superstition . . ."

"Help! I need your help!"

Kosseff's call suddenly broke their shared moment of fear. Through the one-way mirror they saw Charlie doubled over, writhing in pain. Kosseff was trying to soothe him.

"He's having some kind of seizure!" she called as Maggie and Scully rushed in.

"Get him on his side," Scully ordered while Maggie soothed the boy.

"Charlie, you're going to be okay."

Still behind the one-way mirror, Mulder stood deep in thought. The existence of Michael and the old woman's belief had put everything in a new . . . and unpleasant . . . perspective. Three people had died already. He didn't want there to be any more.

Scully and Mulder met a little later in the corridor outside Charlie Holvey's private room. Night had fallen in the world beyond the brightly lit, antiseptic halls of the hospital, but there was no prospect of going home. They talked as they strolled down the corridor to the coffee machine in the central lobby.

"How's Charlie?" asked Mulder.

"He's resting. What about Mrs. Holvey?"

"I'm amazed that she hasn't broken down completely," Mulder replied. "She's trying to get some sleep in the waiting room."

"The doctors say Charlie had some sort of seizure, but they haven't determined the cause."

Mulder nodded. He had the feeling that it was going to be a long night. The sort of night where you can't wait for the return of the sun. For daylight to banish the fears summoned by darkness . . .

Charlie was half asleep when the nurse came to give him a shot. He started as she touched his arm.

"It's okay, Charlie," she soothed. "I didn't mean to scare you. I'm Nurse Castor."

Charlie stared at her as she opened an alcohol swab and grabbed his arm.

"Charlie, I'm just going to give you something that will help you sleep."

"I don't want a shot," Charlie said sulkily.

"But that's what happens when you spit out your medicine," explained Nurse Castor, cleaning off a spot on his arm. "We have to give it to you some other way. I promise you it won't hurt."

"No," protested Charlie.

Castor readied the syringe, holding the boy's arm securely. He was squirming now, trying to pull away.

"No! Don't do it. Don't do it!" Charlie cried—but not to the nurse. He was looking past her, at the darkness behind the door. Only it wasn't dark now. Something was glowing there, taking shape. Another boy, exactly like Charlie, but with evil in his face. The dead twin. Michael.

He took one step forward, then another.

"Charlie, now, I want you to behave!" the nurse instructed sternly, ignoring Charlie's efforts to free himself. She couldn't see what he saw.

Michael was picking up a metal rod from a stand, raising it higher and higher as he advanced on the nurse . . .

"No, Michael! Don't!" Charlie screamed, and finally Nurse Castor turned—as the metal rod came down upon her head. Surprised, she barely had time to raise her hands, sucking breath for a scream that never came. Her body thudded to the floor an instant later, and the hypodermic rolled under the bed.

Chapter Eleven

Somehow Maggie had managed to fall asleep, curled up on the couch in the waiting room, despite the loudspeaker's constant calls requesting doctors and nurses to respond to the emergencies and occurrences of a hospital at night.

She came awake groggily at a tug on her arm. It was Charlie doing the tugging. He was fully dressed and seemed to be okay.

"I want to go home now," he said flatly.

"Charlie?" she said, a little dazed. "What are you doing up? Why are you dressed?"

"They said I could go home now."

"Who said that?" asked Maggie.

"The doctors," Charlie stated. "They said I could leave."

Still a little dazed and a bit suspicious,

Maggie searched his face. He seemed to be all right. But it was odd . . .

"All right then," she said hesitantly. "Let's just get your coat. And we'll talk to the doctors."

"No, Mommy!" Charlie demanded, tugging at her. "Let's just go home."

Maggie felt a cold fear as he touched her, a fear that she forced herself to dismiss. She was his mother. Charlie needed her. Fighting against a deep instinct that said everything was wrong, she reached out and took his hand.

"Okay, Charlie. We'll go straight home."

The central staircase landing above the hospital lobby was a good place to keep an eye on everything. Scully stood there thinking about their next move as Mulder went down to get another cup of coffee from the machine. Munchausen by proxy had been pretty well demolished, but there had to be some other rational explanation.

Idly she looked out through the window at

the parking lot. Then with more concentration, her interest suddenly aroused. Seeing her look out, Mulder stopped sipping his coffee and came up the stairs.

"What are you looking at?" he asked.

"Is that Mrs. Holvey?" asked Scully, pointing. Down one side of the shadowed lot a woman was walking quickly, leading a young boy by the hand. They stopped next to the car Scully was certain belonged to Maggie.

"There," she said, pointing again. "I think she's got Charlie with her."

Mulder didn't need to see any more. Abandoning his coffee on the windowsill, he leaped for the stairs to the wards, Scully after him.

In the doorway to Charlie's room they stopped suddenly. Charlie lay in his bed. He looked sick, his breathing weak and shallow. But he was definitely there.

Scully looked at Mulder, confused. She was sure she'd seen Maggie and Charlie. It had definitely been their car . . .

A low groan on the other side of the bed

interrupted her train of thought. A nurse lay there, bleeding from the forehead. Scully took one look and dashed to the door, shouting, "Nurse!"

Mulder bent down next to the nurse.

"Are you all right?"

"He hit me," said Nurse Castor, still surprised and bewildered, looking at the blood on her hands that had come away from her forehead.

"Who? Charlie?" asked Scully.

"No. Not him," Castor said. "There were two of them. Two boys."

A nurse came hurrying in then, Mulder and Scully stepping back to give her room. Mulder was the first to react to what Nurse Castor had said.

"You've got to get to Mrs. Holvey's house," he said urgently, steering Scully by the arm toward the hall and elevator.

"Why?" asked Scully, genuinely confused.

"The boy you saw leaving with Mrs. Holvey—it wasn't Charlie."

Scully looked at him, incredulous.

"Mulder, what are you saying? That we just saw Mrs. Holvey leave here with a ghost?"

"A spirit, a ghost, I'm not sure what it is," said Mulder, anxiously pressing the button for the elevator. "But it's what we saw in the photograph. It's what the old woman was trying to protect the family against."

"But Mulder . . ." Scully began, in a last-ditch attempt to offer a serious scientific explanation. Before she could even begin to think what this explanation might be, the elevator arrived with a *ping*, and Mulder practically pushed her into it.

"Whatever it is, it's killed three people, Scully. You've got to get to Mrs. Holvey before it happens again."

"What are you going to do?" asked Scully, uncertain. She felt like she was being swept away by Mulder yet again, his fervent belief overriding her common sense.

"Get help," said Mulder as the elevator doors closed.

Chapter Twelve

Maggie spooned the spaghetti onto the plate with deliberate care, her whole body tense with the thought . . . the suspicion . . . that was growing in her. Charlie—she had to believe it was Charlie—sat in his usual place at the end of the kitchen table. Impassive, silent. But she could feel him watching her, felt that unblinking stare.

She took the plate over and set it down in front of him, trying not to meet his gaze.

"There you go, Charlie."

"Aren't you going to have some, Mommy?" asked Charlie. His voice sounded almost normal, but there was a tinge of something else there. The hint of dark amusement, as if he was baiting her. Or was she imagining it? . . .

"No, dear. I'm not hungry."

She wished that she had listened more to her mother. Paid more attention to the rituals. She could remember only the simple ones. But that would be enough to find out if . . . if Charlie wasn't Charlie, but something else.

Calming herself, she walked slowly to the kitchen drawer where she kept odds and ends, scrabbling in it, trying not to look at him. Trying not to reveal her fear to . . . to whoever was sitting there with her in the kitchen.

"Tomorrow can we go to the park?" the boy asked. His voice was almost gloating now, reveling in her discomfort. In her fear.

Maggie suppressed a shudder, her fingers closing on the box of matches she'd been looking for.

"Yes. Sure," she replied, artificially bright.

"Can I have . . . a balloon?"

"Uh . . . huh," she responded, unable to get any more words out.

"And can we ride the train . . . Mommy?"

It took all her strength not to scream in answer to that, but she bottled it up, holding the box of matches in a tight fist. She even managed a smile as she walked past.

"Now you finish up and Mommy will be right back, okay?"

She didn't look back.

Charlie watched her, though, head pivoting to follow her exit. His mouth twitched a little, as if tasting something, even though he hadn't touched his food.

Maggie was trembling all over as she entered her mother's room, hands shaking as she lit the candles on either side of the brass bowl. It still had some liquid in it.

Composing herself, Maggie uttered the short prayer she had learned long ago in Romania. She spoke it in Romanian, automatically translating it in her head into English, as she'd had to do the other way when she first came to America.

"Blessed waters that flow from the holy rivers. Clear my sight so I may see the evil."

Halfway through, she lit a match and

tossed it into the bowl, quickly following it with two more.

"Please, God. Don't let it be true."

The matches fizzled in the liquid, bobbing up to float on the surface. For a moment Maggie felt relief flood through her.

Then the first match sank, and the second. Finally the third disappeared without a trace.

And the door behind her slowly opened, a chill breeze coming from inside the house.

"What are you doing, Mommy?" asked the thing she now knew wasn't Charlie. It was the spirit of her dead son Michael, infused with evil. The killer of nearly her entire family.

She almost couldn't bear to look at this thing that had taken the image of her much-loved son. Now that she knew what it was, it looked less like Charlie.

As if hearing her thoughts, an unearthly wind suddenly ruffled the spirit's hair, and its mouth twitched, mocking her.

Instinctively she picked up Golda's knife and held it before her, long-forgotten words rising to her mind, her voice weakly chanting.

"*Voi ilelor . . . maistrelor . . . dusmanele omenilor . . . Stapinele vintulu . . .*"

She tried to be strong, but deep in her heart she quailed, knowing she had neither the power nor the knowledge to stand long against this force of ancient evil . . .

Mulder was waiting for the Calusari in the hospital corridor outside Charlie's room. There were four of them this time, led by the elder. They strode into the room together. As he passed, the elder said to Mulder, "Guard the door."

Inside, they quickly set up candles about the bed and placed a number of small jars on the bedside table. Then one of them opened Charlie's pajama top, to reveal his bare chest.

Still the boy slept, seemingly unaware of the powers that were gathering about him. Apparently unaware of the confrontation that was to come . . .

x   x   x

The Holvey house was completely dark. Scully tried the switch by the front door as she entered, but nothing happened.

"Mrs. Holvey?" she called.

There was no answer. Switching on her flashlight, Scully moved farther in, probing the darkness with her thin beam of light.

A heavy thud suddenly sounded up above—as if someone was moving furniture. Scully trained the light upstairs. Whoever . . . whatever . . . had made that noise was up there. Up in Golda's bedroom. Where the old lady had died earlier that day.

Scully started up the stairs, moving cautiously. She didn't like the look of this at all. Maggie's car was parked out front, so she and Charlie had to be here somewhere . . .

Chapter Thirteen

The Calusari began to chant, their low, resonant voices filling the hospital room with a constant sound. The candles flickered, casting crazy shadows on the walls. Mulder stood near the door, uncertain what he could do to help. Choosing to stay out of the way seemed the best thing for the moment.

The Calusari elder placed a bowl on the bedside table, still leading the chant, the others echoing his words. Another Calusari cast rock salt over the boy, the white crystals sparkling as they fell. When they touched his bare skin, he suddenly started awake, hissing. His open eyes did not look like a normal boy's.

The elder took up the first of his bottles and added a powdered herb to the bowl, the chant continuing.

"Voi ilelor . . . maistrelor . . . dusmanele omenilor . . ."

The water hissed and bubbled as the powder hit, and Charlie hissed too—a long, drawn-out "Sssssssss" full of hatred and venom.

The elder added mugwort to the water, and it hissed again. Charlie began to moan, the sound strangely distorted, seeming to come from many directions at once.

"Stapinele vintulu . . . doamnele pamintulu . . . de prin vazduh sburati . . ."

Charlie's moans grew louder, and less and less childlike. His eyes opened wider, staring, lips curling back from feral teeth. He spoke in Romanian, his voice not the voice of a little boy.

"You have no power here!" the spirit within him warned.

The Calusari ignored the voice. They held him now, gripping his arms and head with effort, sweat dripping from their hands and foreheads. Animal growls came from deep inside Charlie, awful sounds, like beasts feeding . . .

The elder sprinkled a red powder into the bowl, and the water turned a deep blood-red. As the color washed through, Charlie screamed, body arching despite the men holding him down.

"You cannot do this!" he spat and howled. "You will be killed by your own tools!"

Mulder flinched, not understanding the words or in fact much else that was happening, but his instinct telling him he should intervene. The elder saw him and beckoned for him to help, pointing at the boy's flailing legs. Even four grown men couldn't hold the boy down now, the evil in him stronger than his physical form.

Hesitantly Mulder grabbed Charlie by the ankles . . . and looked up to meet a gaze that had nothing human in it at all. It saw him, a deep growl welling up as if it had suddenly spotted prey.

"Look away!" cried the elder urgently. "Look away! Or it will recognize you!"

Mulder snapped his eyes away, refocusing on the walls. He felt drained, weakened by the momentary confrontation. It took a second before he realized that the walls were dripping with a golden-brown liquid as thick as honey. It was oozing out everywhere, as if the room itself were sweating.

Mulder looked back as the elder drew a long ceremonial knife. Like the one Golda had, but larger and more ornate, with well-polished gold on its hilt. Brandishing it, the old man moved closer to where another Calusari held out the boy's hand.

As the knife descended, the bed began to vibrate and rise from the floor. Charlie's thrashing grew wilder still, and the moans and growls multiplied, became more distorted, harder to listen to, harder to bear . . .

Scully pushed open the door to Golda's room and slipped in. Instantly a strange wind rose up, loose papers whirling past her, the windows rattling, the stained-glass swastika flapping as if it might burst free.

She could hear a voice—Maggie's voice—but the beam of the flashlight showed no one in the room. Scully moved farther in, following the noise, light flickering over the broken furniture strewn all around.

Finally she moved the beam up toward the ceiling—and found Maggie. She was pressed by some unseen force up against the ceiling, her eyes closed, lips still desperately whispering a protective chant . . .

"Voi ilelor . . . maistrelor . . . dusmancle omenilor . . . stapinele vintulu . . . doamnele . . ."

Aghast, Scully moved closer—and a shadow flitted across the far corner of the room, just at the edge of her sight. She turned, but it was gone. Then it was on the other side, flicking past. The shadow of a boy . . .

"Charlie!"

Whatever it was answered through Maggie's lips, the boyish voice gone strange and horrible, emanating from somewhere within the stricken woman.

"Mommy?"

The shadow moved again, and Scully turned to the windows—as they suddenly blew in, the stained-glass swastika exploding with them, showering Scully's upraised arms with broken glass.

Immediately something moved behind her and Scully wheeled, reaching for her pistol— only to be picked up and thrown across the room by an unseen force.

She landed hard, the flashlight skittering away from her. No gun could help her now. Nothing could help her now . . . not even Mulder.

Chapter Fourteen

The hospital bed had risen at least a foot now, and Charlie looked even less human. His stomach was distended, blown up like a balloon— as if something inside was trying to get out.

He spoke again, voice distorted but easily understandable to the Calusari. The Romanian words were meaningless to Mulder, but he heard the hatred and the threats, the power in them chilling his blood.

"I will come for you at night. You cannot escape."

The elder ignored him, the knife still descending. Then, with great effort, he drew its sharp blade across the boy's open palm, catching the blood in a small earthenware bowl.

"It hurts!" cried Charlie, his voice suddenly like a normal boy's.

Disturbed, Mulder let go of the boy's legs, suddenly unsure about whether they should continue. None of the Calusari moved, but the elder snapped at Mulder.

"Do not let go! He tricks you!"

Obediently Mulder tightened his grip. He was out of his depth with this, but had the sense to know it. All he could do was place his trust in the Calusari. More lives than his depended on it. Scully, wherever she was, and Maggie Holvey . . .

Satisfied, the elder returned to his task, pouring the collected blood into the larger bowl. Taking up a white rooster feather, he dipped it into the bloody, bubbling concoction, and using the feather as a brush, he began to paint the reverse swastika on the boy's heaving, bloated chest.

For a second Scully didn't know where she was, pain hazing her mind. She seemed to be on the floor somewhere . . . then she heard Maggie, still chanting, still pinned to the ceiling.

She remembered. The Holvey house. The

dead twin . . . and there he was, emerging from the darkness, a fiend in the shape of a boy. He held Golda's knife above his head in both hands and was coming toward her for the killing blow. There was nothing, nothing she could do except raise her arm in a last, instinctive, useless—

Many voices came from Charlie now, voices screaming and threatening, howling and moaning. Pain and anger, fear and hatred, all mixed together in a terrible cacophony . . . surely too much for the small body of the boy to hold. Too much evil, evil still fighting . . .

Then the elder of the Calusari painted the last of the four dots between the spokes of the swastika and all the voices merged into one last, frenzied scream as the bed fell back to the floor.

The Calusari stopped chanting. Charlie's stomach returned to its usual shape, his eyes rolling back for a moment before they closed in normal sleep.

Mulder let go of Charlie's feet and stepped back.

It was over.

The knife whistled down, the boy's twisted, evil face the last thing Scully believed she would ever see. Then he was gone, and the knife clattered on the floor. At the same time, Maggie slid down the wall to land in a crumpled heap.

Quickly Scully moved over to her.

"Are you all right?"

Maggie looked at Scully, sharing the moment of rescue with her, the moment both thought would never come. Then she said, "Charlie . . ."

There was a question in her tone, a question Scully didn't understand till she saw the pile of ash in the middle of the floor. Were both boys dead now? The one who always should have been, and poor Charlie?

Mulder was waiting for them at the hospital, watching the boy. The elder watched too.

"Let the boy rest," he pronounced. "We must find the mother. The boy needs her."

As if answering him, Scully and Maggie

came through the door. Mulder looked at them wearily, pleased that his partner seemed to be all right. He asked anyway.

"Scully, are you okay?"

"We're okay," Scully answered. "How's Charlie?"

"My son?" Maggie asked, seeing him lying on the bed. "Charlie! It's okay!"

She flew to the bed, taking Charlie's hand, the relief evident in her face. Mulder and Scully watched for a moment, till the elder of the Calusari beckoned them out into the corridor.

"It is over, for now," he said to Mulder, a deep concern in his wise face. "But you must be careful. It knows you."

Mulder nodded. He would remember what had happened that night. And the warning.

Recorded annotation to X-file
"The Calusari"
by Agent Fox Mulder

The strange case of Charlie Holvey and the deaths that occurred during his possession by a dark and malevolent force are unsolved. The boy, who will celebrate his tenth birthday next month, remains under the watchful care of his mother. And though I believe him innocent of the crimes, I am disturbed by the warnings of the Calusari: that neither innocence nor vigilance may be protection against the howling heart of evil.

Read the next book in the
X-Files Young Adult Series:

The X-Files #2: **EVE**
by Ellen Steiber

Chapter One

The tree-lined streets of Greenwich, Connecticut, blazed with autumn color. The maple leaves were a deep red, the oak leaves golden, and the sky a crisp, clear blue. A whirl of fallen leaves spun by on a cold wind, and Donna Watkins pulled up the collar of her navy blue warm-up suit. She and her husband, Ted, had been jogging for nearly twenty minutes. Usually she'd be sweating by now, but today she just couldn't get warm. Beneath her wool gloves, her fingers were icy. She felt chilled to the bone.

Winter's coming early this year, Donna thought uneasily. Although it was still early in November, many of the trees had already lost their leaves. Their black branches clutched the sky like skeletal fingers. Donna shivered at the sight. She didn't know why, but bare branches always made her think of death.

Donna picked up the pace as they cut across the street and rounded the corner onto their own block. Ted waved at one of their neighbors, Mr. Whelan, who was raking leaves. Mr. Whelan looked perfectly cheerful. Donna tried to shake off her uneasy feeling. After all, it was a beautiful Saturday morning, and she and Ted had recently moved into their dream house. They'd looked for a long time before finding a home in Greenwich. Neither of them wanted to live in one of those suburbs where all the houses were identical and most looked as if they'd been built in an afternoon. Donna loved this neighborhood with its huge trees, wide streets, spacious old homes, and neatly trimmed lawns. There was something reassuring about Greenwich—the sense that everything was in order. Here, things were exactly as they should be.

Donna slowed her pace as she heard a dog barking in alarm. Later she would remember the dog's bark as the first sign that something was wrong.

She glanced across the street and saw a young girl standing at the end of a circular drive that led to a large, white two-story house. It was Teena Simmons, their neighbor's daughter. She was coatless and shivering, dressed only in a short-sleeved white blouse, pink shorts, and white anklets. She was holding on to a stuffed rabbit.

"What's she doing there by herself?" Donna asked, breathing hard.

Ted shrugged, equally puzzled. Together they crossed the street to find out.

"Teena?" Ted called.

"Honey?" Donna asked, her voice concerned. The eight-year-old girl had seemed quiet when they had met her a few weeks earlier; but this was more than shyness. Although they were standing right next to her, Teena didn't answer. She wouldn't even look at them. She just stood there shivering. There was something distant in her manner, as if she hadn't heard them. It was the second sign that something was wrong. Seriously wrong.

"You're freezing," Donna said gently. She wondered if the girl was in shock. "Where's your jacket?"

Teena remained silent, hugging her stuffed toy.

"Where's your daddy?" Ted asked.

For the first time, Teena spoke. "In the backyard," she said. "He told me he needed some time to himself."

The couple exchanged puzzled glances.

"I'd say his time's up," Ted said, starting toward the back of the house.

"C'mon, hon," Donna said to the girl. "I'm sure your daddy wouldn't want you to catch cold."

Ted walked around the side of the house to the backyard. He passed a few lawn chairs, a barbecue grill, and a redwood bird feeder. He made his way to the far end of the yard, where Joel Simmons had set up a small playground with swings and a mini-slide.

Joel Simmons was sitting on one of the swings, his back to Ted. He was wearing dark green coveralls.

He was probably doing some yard work and wanted to take a break, Ted figured, not as worried as he'd been a few moments before. "Joel?" he called.

There was no answer.

"Hey, Joel," Ted said, trying to keep it light. "I thought that swing set was supposed to be for your daughter, not you."

But there was still no response from Joel Simmons.

"What the—?" Ted murmured. He moved toward the swings, unaware that Donna and Teena had followed him into the yard.

He gave Joel a friendly smack on the back.

Joel's body swung slightly. Then his head dropped sharply to one side.

Ted felt his heart begin to race. Joel was unnaturally pale, his skin a sickening bluish white. A thin line of blood trickled from the corner of his mouth, and there were two angry-looking puncture wounds in the side of his neck. His eyes were open, staring up blankly, frozen in eternal shock.

Ted jumped as Teena let out an anguished scream. Donna pulled the girl close, shielding her from the sight of her father's grisly corpse.

Stunned, Ted backed away from the body, then began running toward the house. "I'll call 911," he shouted to his wife.

Donna stood by the side of the house, holding on to Teena. The girl was sobbing, her head buried against Donna, her whole body shaking. Donna thought her heart would break when Teena looked toward the swings and whispered, "Daddy."

Donna's world had changed. Minutes earlier Greenwich had felt safe—a place where everything was exactly as it should be. Now that sense of order was gone. And she knew she'd never truly feel safe again.

The winter wind blew, and Joel Simmons's dead body swung like a macabre puppet on the child's swing set.